The
SUBSTANCE
Of
FORGETTING

The
SUBSTANCE
Of
FORGETTING

Kristjana Gunnars

Red Deer College Press

THE PUBLISHERS
Red Deer College Press
56 Avenue & 32 Street Box 5005
Red Deer Alberta Canada T4N 5H5

CREDITS
Design by Alex Hass, Hodgson + Haas Design Associates
Cover Photo by Chick Rice, Vancouver
Author Photo by W.C. Christie
Printed & Bound in Canada by Best Gagné Printing Ltée for Red
Deer College Press

ACKNOWLEDGEMENTS
The publishers gratefully acknowledge the financial contribution
of the Alberta Foundation for the Arts, Alberta Culture and Mul-
ticulturalism, The Canada Council and Red Deer College.

CANADIAN CATALOGUING IN PUBLICATION DATA
Gunnars, Kristjana, 1948-
The substance of forgetting
ISBN 0-88995-085-7 (bound)
ISBN 0-88995-092-X (pbk.)
I. Title
PS8563.U57S8   1992   C813'.54   C92-091326-1
PR9199.3.G85S8   1992

All networks of possible meaning must be exhausted beneath common sense, banal, vulgar, obvious meaning, or cruel, threatening, and aggressive meaning—before we can understand that they are ungraspable, that they adhere to no axis, that they are "arbitrary" just like the sign, the name, and the utterance, but also pleasure and jouissance.

—JULIA KRISTEVA,
Desire and Language

I will arise and go now, and go to Innisfree,
And a small cabin build there, of clay and wattles made;
Nine bean-rows will I have there, a hive for the honey-bee,
And live alone in the bee-loud glade.

And I shall have some peace there, for peace comes dropping slow,
Dropping from the veils of the morning....
—W.B. YEATS,
"The Lake Isle of Innisfree"

The
SUBSTANCE
Of
FORGETTING

I WOULD SAY I AM TIRED. I THOUGHT I COULD HARDLY GET more tired and then I did. The quiet hours drip. I watch them in the melting snow on the quince plants and juniper bushes. The snow here in the hills above Wood Lake was once four feet deep. The snow was piled up against my windows thick and warm. Then it melted and started dripping into slow puddles clogged in the potholes of the road I call my street. The lethargic drops hang from the balcony railing as if they were translucent pregnant spiders.

There is so much fog in the valley that I cannot see the lake below the house. When I look up the mountain into the pine trees they are bathed in the milk-white dream of the mist. The tops of the trees are lost in cloud.

We have been dreaming too much, the forest and I. When I walk up the old wagon trail toward Mission the woods close in on me. Jack pines push onto the road and the ponderosas stand spread with upward bending limbs as if conducting the dreams I dream in the mist.

.

I think I have been mesmerized by the fog. There is nothing to see when you stare into the gray thickness except your own visions.

.

The lake has been frozen for two months. White ribbons lace the gray surface of the ice. They are the ripples of snow the wind has blown together. By the highway ice fishermen are sitting in lawn chairs beside a hole in the ice. Their fishing lines go down the hole. Thermoses lean against the chair legs. Further out what looks like a heron stands waiting. There will be fish debris when the catch is gutted. Another heron waits down the lake. Their long legs are thin and exposed, their long necks stiff. They follow every movement of the ice fishermen. At the boat launch a puddle has formed on the ice. A duck tries desperately to swim in the shallow water.

.

When the clouds roll in at the end of autumn they stay snug in the Okanagan Valley for five months. Sometimes the clouds are so low they touch the water. Then they are like a shunned lover lowering for a slight touch of the beautiful earth. Sometimes they rise to the tops of the hills and look down on the forests. Then they are like a captor guarding its prey.

The clouds make me sad. They remind me of what I am not doing, what I am not saying. But I think *in a short while it will be blossom time*. Then I look forward to blossom time and my mind wanders into dream. In my dream all things are in bloom. Apple blossoms, apricot blossoms, cherry blossoms.

.

Somehow life has thrown me on this hillside in the receding tide. In this gentlest land possible I only want to desire the hour of clarity in the lake when the forest can see its face in the water. I only want to long for the moment of a break in the clouds when the red sunlight leaks onto the sandy hills and they are luminescent orange in a burst of light.

.

I have never known such fog. How it creeps onto the valley floor in the late evening. Suddenly the lake is bathed in a thick veil. By morning the valley is filled. The darkness is impenetrable. No light shines anywhere. The hills are nude and asleep, engulfed in a substance of forgetting.

Day crawls over slow day. The frozen water, the crystal-packed soil, the ice-rained jack pines would have us think there is no time. Just a slow succession of light and darkness of concern to no one. There is nowhere to go. No obligations remain. Even the train that whistles as it rounds the corner of Kalamalka's south end is silent and seems not to have any errands in the mountains anymore.

ONE

"YOU ARE BEAUTIFUL, MADAME." I WOULD LIKE TO BEGIN with that. *You are beautiful, madame*. Just like that. Those words must be spoken in semidarkness. The lights are off. It is night. The curtains are slightly parted and light from a streetlamp outside filters into the room. The room is full of dark blue light because the curtains are blue. Perhaps we are breaking all the rules. Perhaps we are together because Jules is a Québec separatist and we are in the United States. Nothing should fit. Nothing should be reasonable. During the day we were going somewhere, walking from one place to another. It is immaterial where we are going except that we had to go. "What does Québec want?" Whether I asked that or whether Jules posed a rhetorical question is also unimportant.

Someone asked that and the question was in the air. He tightened the collar of his green coat because the cold wind began to blow just then. He answered the question with deliberation. He may even have gesticulated with his right hand in the American air. "Québec wants a free and independent Québec in a strong and united Canada," he asserted. There may have been newly fallen snow outside and I was surprised to find his eyes were blue. I said so. Even though his hair was dark his eyes were blue. "No. My eyes are usually red from reading too much," he said. I imagined his eyes red. Perhaps we can color reality the way we want to. Perhaps we can deny what we see with our eyes and substitute what we see with our desire. It was the quiet of the morning and we were about to go somewhere, probably to airports and into airplanes to fly in different directions. There were time restrictions. There was a closed-in feeling. "Do you really live in the country?" he asked me. I nodded. He would go home to the city thinking I live deep in the mountains, away from urban things. It was not exactly untrue. It was not exactly true. It is the question the writer asks when writing a book: Shall I fill in all the details? Or shall I let the reader imagine them all? Who should write this book, me or my reader? What if I give you dots and numbers and you draw in the lines? Perhaps he would imagine my horse, my German Shepherd, my truck. Chickens and pigs even. Or he would think up my solitary log cabin with nothing but a parrot hanging from the ceiling. No dogs, no animals. Or he would not imagine anything. There would be a blank, never filled in, forgotten tomorrow.

TWO

I HAVE A COTTAGE IN THE OKANAGAN. THAT AT LEAST IS simple and clear. Not as exotic as having had a farm in Kenya, say, but it is a simpler thing.

First I thought of it as a house. An estate with land. I said I had a house on a mountain with a view. It was true. My cottage is on the mountainside but the mountain is small and hilly. From my windows I see Wood Lake and Kalamalka Lake and the mountains on the other side. There are orchards on the lower part of the hills and pine forests above. Between the pine forests are open stretches of green. As you go further south the open land becomes more frequent. There it is brown and barren.

Then I saw the cedar on the outside wall was warping. There were holes. The front porch was sinking. The windowsills were homemade. The house felt wooden and the wood echoed when I walked on the floor. Then the house became a cottage.

·

It was my lovely cottage on the old wagon trail to Mission. Nothing surrounds me but a few other houses, all looking at the lake. All of us here have nowhere to go except into our gardens. We sit at our windows, we rake our lawns, we prune our trees, shovel our snow. Here we are. That is all. We enjoy what we see.

At eight in the morning a few schoolchildren run out of a few of the houses and bunch up at the school bus stop. A yellow bus rattles by, stops and the children are gone. Then some of the restless adults climb into well-built automobiles and drive to town for a job. Sometimes I am one of them. Sometimes I am not.

When I am not, I sit at a wicker table and write a book. As I put words down I watch the sun crawl over the mountain in the east. It rises over the crowns of the pine trees and blares into my cottage rooms. The sun is all around me and I feel warm. I think warm thoughts. I remember warm people.

THREE

JULES WAS SLEEPING AND I WAS THINKING. HIS ARM WAS wrapped tightly around me and the light was blue. There was no sound. In American towns like this no one drove their cars at night. The streets were empty. I could tell the streets were empty from the slight parting of the curtains where the light of the streetlamp filtered in. I thought about things we say. The more you say about a thing the more you destroy it. The best thing I know is silence. I would like to just read his thoughts. Everything he says is beside the point. There is no point. He says more with his blue eyes than with his words yet his eyes are not expressive. They tell me nothing. I am imagining everything. I am climbing down a ladder. The ladder goes around and around a tower and I am climbing down to the ground. When I am on the ground I know I will look up and on the uppermost balcony of the tower I will see his figure. He will be bending over and looking down at me. He is wearing a dark hat and a large coat that trails almost to the ground. It is so dark that I cannot tell if the coat is green. Only a little moonlight filters through the broken clouds. I can hear a simpering wind in the branches. The branches are barren because it is winter. The branches are naked, wrapped in a sheet of snow. Their arms tightly grip each other. The trees are sleeping until spring. Then there will be little green buds. The green knots will untie and leaves will form. But I do not think about spring. I am aware of the dark figure high overhead observing me from a great distance. I am cold. Snow is everywhere and my feet are wet. The wind penetrates my paltry clothing. The man on the tower has told so many stories and I remember them all. They are enchanting as fairy tales, stricken and tragic as wartime dramas, simple and clear as children's stories. They lead into the woods where I cannot follow. I begin to climb down the ladder. When I stumble he grabs my waist and holds me up. It is only a moment. In the moonlight I see his face for the first time. His face tells me nothing. I know I have to run. If I do not run I will hear too much. The wind will grow louder and the figure above will begin to call. I know I will not like hearing his voice calling. If he calls me back and I try to climb the ladder again the ladder will disappear. There will be no tower. The structure will always be too distant. Like the moon it will follow me when I go away and recede from me when I approach. I think the figure in the green coat will hide his stories from me. I will try to hear them and there will be no telling. Then I will try not to hear them. But when you try not to hear stories they come out all around you anyway. Suddenly you hear things you never wanted to know. You want everyone to stop talking, to take away those words. Everyone is talking too much. I begin to hurry away. There is a path in the snow, a path leading to the hotel. I follow the trail and stumble when it winds. I can see the hotel beyond the naked woods. The massive stone structure towers over the tallest trees. I hear music from the ballroom. Lights are on everywhere. I run into the foyer, knowing the dark figure on the gray tower is still looking down. He could be thinking anything. I cannot tell what he is thinking. I am glad to be back among the many people in their fine clothes with crystal wine glasses in their hands. I greet them elegantly. As elegantly as I can with my wet feet and paltry clothes. I go into my room and bathe in the warm water I find there. I lie down in the large bed. The night was dark. Through the slight parting in the curtain I saw snow. The snow went around in flurries outside the window. The light of a streetlamp filtered into the room. The curtains were blue and the light was blue. Jules was sleeping. His arm was wrapped tightly around me.

FOUR

I KNOW I HAVE WANTED TO SAY THESE THINGS FOR A LONG time. Years even. To write letters that would explain everything. Then I see there is nothing to explain. The snow is melting at the edges of my driveway and nothing needs to be explained. When I look I find there is no one to take the words that would set everything right. There is no right and wrong. That is what I was also thinking as the snow flurried in circles in the light of the streetlamp. Perhaps we have broken all the rules but it does not matter. Right and wrong do not matter. It does not matter whether the man sleeping is my lover or not. No one cares who he is. Everything is easy, much easier than I thought. Something else matters instead. Jules came to me and said he had no flowers. *I have no flowers*. Apologetic because he was French and should bring flowers but I saw he was not afraid. I was not afraid either. Somehow it matters that we were not afraid. It matters because it will be much easier to take my bags to the city now. I do not even have to bring my bags. I can leave them under the apricot trees in the valley. There are always new bags to be had, new things to put in them. When the snow flurried in circles I saw it is a confused and angry world. I like to think we are not afraid in it. Like the snow we fall where we may. We fall into each other's arms. I wanted to fall like that because it is cold and the snow is coming down and I am in a strange American town. It is a strange town because it is like all other towns. They are all the same and I am confused when I try to find north and south. It does not matter which direction we go in. Knowing that, I take my bag and go home. I see no signs of Jules as I go. He has disappeared into the white air like the flakes of snow. There will never be a sign of him and it does not matter. I can take my bag and watch it come out of a trapdoor in the wall at the airport. Coming home is easy. I am happy when the airplane lands in the valley. The grass is green and there is no snow between the mountains. I drive along the lakes and see that the ice has melted while I was away. The lights on the hills are reflected in the water that has found a new release in the warm days. I am happy the ice has melted. I like to see the water move in ripples. I like to see if a wind is blowing by looking at the lake from my window. I have learned to read the stories on the surface of the lake and in the color of the water. What I wanted to be able to say is such a small thing, nothing consequential. How peaceful it is to see. I thought of all the years we wanted to say things and then there was no language for them. Even if we had the language we would not have known how to use it. I must get a dictionary and begin at the beginning, at the first word. There is something in the language I do not understand. I could only say this is a language that is not my own. Now it does not matter.

FIVE

IT WAS AUGUST WHEN I FIRST CAME TO MY COTTAGE. THE
sun was shining every day. It was hot. Flowers continu-
ally bloomed. On my land all the apricot trees were
covered with fruit. The trees were old and their branches grew in all directions. On every branch were thousands of apricots. The fruit made the branches heavy
and they drooped toward the ground. In the morning I
went out and stood among my apricot trees. How could
I pick all these apricots? If I picked them what could be
done with them? Where do they go? As the late summer days came and went I plucked the small yellow-
brown fruit and put them in a blue bucket. Soon there
were many buckets full. I washed the apricots, cut them
in half, took the pits out and filled freezer bags with
halved fruit. Soon the freezer was full of such bags. I

put apricot halves in cooking pots and boiled them with sugar. Soon many jars of apricot jam were everywhere. I had never seen so much food coming into my house for free. Soon there were large bottles of apricot chutney. A friend faxed me recipes for apricot wine. When I slept at night I even dreamed apricots. I was not prepared for such a great harvest.

Roberta and Justine came from Vancouver. In the morning they were outside picking apricots. They were laughing. Around them hung the heavy branches. No matter how much we picked, there always seemed to be equally many apricots left on the trees. Roberta and Justine picked and washed and cut and froze apricots until they were silly. At the end of the day they fell into chairs on the balcony, took a glass of cold wine from the Grey Monk cellars further up the hill and laughed in their exhaustion. Their laughter rang like Indian wedding bells over the water.

My friend Hillary came from Edmonton. She too went out to pick the endless fruit. She brought blue buckets filled to the brim into the kitchen. When I woke in the morning I would find her cooking apricot halves into jam at my stove. She cooked a potful and burned it. She tried again and cooked another potful. The jam burned again. "I'm not going to quit until I make successful jam," she insisted. I said she was welcome to make many successful jams. There were apricots enough for a thousand tests. One day I came home from work at five in the afternoon. There she stood proudly with six new jars of successful jam. We celebrated her success with more Grey Monk wine.

My friend David came from Calgary. It was not possible to process more apricots. They were falling from the trees faster than I could pick them. David and I began to shovel the fruit off the ground. We filled garbage bags full of dented and rotting apricots. Every shovelful filled the air with the odor of apricot blossoms, wine, perfume. The bags were heavy. We hauled them up to the road to be picked up. David lifted the bags onto a wheelbarrow and pushed the wheelbarrow strenuously up the steep hill. He breathed hard and exhausted because he was a smoker. "I came here for a vacation and instead I'm going to die of overwork," he declared. But he did not die of exhaustion. No matter how many bags we took to the road or how many we filled with fallen fruit, the ground was forever littered with the same number of apricots. Every time one was picked up another fell from the tree to take its place. The fruit lay rotting and fermenting. We gave up. We had more Grey Monk wine and laughed at our failure to make a dent in the piles of fruit all over my land. In the end I sat on my front steps and looked at the mess of fruit on the ground and the thousands still on the trees. The air was filled with the smell of fermenting apricots. I knew I could not even give my fruit away.

Everyone in the valley was faced with the same over-load. I could not put a sign on the highway pointing to my house. A sign that said U-PICK. APRICOTS. FREE. The highway was too far from my house. Not even tourists would come up the hill for them.

Down the road a ways was a honey farm, the Raykar honey farm. When you walked past, the air smelled of penetrating bitter honey. Little bee hives dotted the acreages. Across the road bees could be seen blithely searching for nectar.

The bees found my fermenting apricots. As I sat on my steps with my chin in my palm, feeling the heat of the afternoon sun in my bones, I saw the bees discover the fallen fruit. For them it was paradise. Soon there were hundreds of bees. Thousands of bees. They buzzed in the fermenting fruit every day, at all times. I walked among the thousands of bees and they were in no way concerned about me. I knew they would never sting. If I put my hand in the swarm of bees on the ground they simply buzzed irritably in an effort to make me go away so they could drink more nectar. They were happy. When I heard them flying from clump to clump I learned to recognize the sound of bee happiness.

Soon I realized all the bees were drunk. There was alcohol in the fermenting fruit pulp and the bees drank endlessly of the riches of the earth. They flew sideways, without direction, buzzing silly and dazed, droning dizzily, no longer comprehending a thing. My little orchard rang with laughter.

SIX

JUSTINE WAS BATHING IN THE WATERS OF KALAMALKA LAKE just below my cottage. She spread her arms and hands over the surface the water. A cry of delight sounded from her now and then. She called out exclamations in French.

Roberta watched her from a blanket on the grass. She was sitting with her knees in her arms and sunglasses over her eyes. A slight smile was on her lips. She was reflecting on her widowhood, carrying a tinge of sadness with her.

I lay on the grass on my back. I was looking up into the blue sky. I was wondering how it could be. *I am not even on vacation*, I said to myself. *This is my everyday life.*

SEVEN

TIMES LIKE THIS THE WORLD RECEDES. I AM FLOATING. ALL IS
a strange thin haze and I am floating between silk-gray
water and down-gray clouds. The clouds are broken.
They are torn and strands of their insides lie scattered
across the sky. I am looking at the thin leftovers of
cloud and I am floating. All is memory and memory
deceives. There is nothing to know. Nothing I might
know would change anything. There is no reason to
change anything. When I breathe, the torn clouds are
in my chest. Little fluffs of insulation float in my lungs.
I am insulated from the world by my memory. The
sweetness, the bitterness, the nothingness of my memory. Now that I am floating in the remnants of clouds I
remember everything I have ever done. My actions are
strange to me. I do not recognize myself in my actions.

They did not come from me. My life has not been lived by me. It was someone else who did all those things. It was not me Jules lay down with in the snow. The wind was cold and he was there but I was somewhere else. Perhaps I was here between the velvet water and silk clouds. Perhaps I only dreamed him. I dreamed him because he is familiar to me yet I know he is a stranger. Everyone tells me he is a stranger. I no longer remember who is familiar and who is strange. All of them melt into one. In my memory it is so warm that they have all blended into one.

I love my memories like I love a good book. But I do not know who wrote the book. A name is on the cover but the name tells me nothing. Jules is in the book, moving through the pages like a thin haze. Something about his voice or his spirit or his presence moves through the words and lines and pages. I do not know where this presence comes from. He did not ask to be there. I did not ask for him to be there. I think if I see him again I will not recognize him. The man in the book is not Jules. He is someone else. He is a stranger. I know he is stranger. I am a stranger in my own memory. I do not recognize myself either.

EIGHT

I DO NOT SLEEP BECAUSE THE HIGHWAY IS BARREN AND OPEN. There is nothing to see for hundreds of miles except snow-covered fields. The wind glides across the miles, chilled and snow laden. I can see drifts of snow accumulating. Tongues of loose snow fly onto the road and off into the stricken grass. I do not sleep because of the stricken grass. I know I must cross the empty fields in the new day. It will be a milk-white day and there will be no sun. I will crawl over the land like a crab at sea bottom. The prairie in the loosening ice of early spring is lonely and uninviting. I already feel the tongues of snow crawling under my skin. The ice looks for places to stick in the corners of my bones. In the new day I see empty vinyl seats, old plastic cups, tin ashtrays where no one has been, chrome door handles that have no fingerprints, car seats unwarmed by human heat. All is untouched. The new day waits, crisp and clear. It waits to be invaded. I do not want to go into that cold reality, stark as a dream I cannot escape. I want to pause here in the arms of a stranger in a strange room. He is imprinting himself onto my memory. The imprint cannot be erased. He is making himself irreversible, tattooing his image on my body forever. He has written this text on my body. A text that stops time in its passing. A text that says halt.

NINE

MY FRIEND DAVID FROM CALGARY HAD HIS FIRST VACATION IN several years. He is the man who cannot stop working. He came to the Okanagan Valley to put his feet up in view of the lakes and mountains. When he found there were too many apricots to keep from relaxing we drove to the north end of the valley and found a houseboat in Sycamous. We drove the houseboat onto the Shuswap Lakes. Here at least there would be no apricots.

We drove the slow boat over the water. Hour after hour went by and the water was gray-blue and the dark green mountains towered on all sides. The water made me glad. The barely perceptible rocking of the boat made me glad. The air was warm. All the world receded into dream. Nothing existed but the tiny rippling waves on the lakes and the bulky mountains.

In the dusk we beached the boat and made a fire on the shore. Behind us was thick impenetrable forest. The water slowed in the falling darkness and began to lap the stones lazily. We had fallen silent too. There was no sound except the crackling branches in the flames. It was curious to me that my home in the valley had so many delights around it. I had never lived in so delightful a place before.

David could not stop working. "We must go out on the lakes where there are no distractions and edit your manuscript," he said. In the early dawn, at four in the morning when the boat was beached at the far end of one of the Shuswap Arms, he was up at the kitchen table working. He was sitting on the bench that was nailed to the wall of the boat kitchen. I got up, made a pot of coffee and sat down to work as well. It was still dark. All the world was as still as a whisper. The bears were all in the woods. We read the pages and made changes to words every now and then. When we spoke our voices marred the quiet of the morning.

For eight hours we concentrated, not noticing time passing. Dawn turned to morning. The sun rose and shone on the water. Once we stepped out and watched the blank stillness of the water. The thick forests of the mountainsides mirrored themselves in the lake.

We read through to the end. When we were finished David drew a deep breath, the kind smokers take after holding their breath for a while. He packed up the manuscript busily and quickly went outside to stand on the deck. He stood watching the water. I was thinking that the author of the text no longer remembers what was reality and what was dream. What was lived and what written. If I write what I have lived I too will think it is just a story. I will forget where the story came from.

TEN

I TOLD DAVID THAT THE OKANAGAN IS THE NAPA VALLEY OF Canada. He should drink the wine made from grapes grown here. We have had too much French wine and American wine. "You should do for Canadian wine what you do for Canadian literature," I said. David believed Canadian literature was as good as anything in the world and should be supported. Canadian books should be bought and read because they tell us about ourselves the way no one else can. "But the wine is too bitter," he said. He would not drink it. "Canadian wine tastes like Diesel fuel," he declared.

"Today I will convince you that you are wrong," I announced one Sunday morning. I drove him to the Grey Monk wine cellars. The Grey Monk estate lay on the other side of the hill. We headed west, up the steep inclines, on a road that wound around in sharp turns and sudden corners. Orchards with billowing fruit trees stretched out everywhere before us. Apple, peach, plum, pear orchards. We ascended the top of the hill and headed down the other side. Suddenly we arrived at the winery. There was a white stucco building that resembled the Spanish-style estates one sees in California. We went inside to a large room where products were displayed. In one corner was a wine tasting bar. Off to the side was the bottling plant. Along the wall were huge windows with a view of Okanagan Lake deep below. We went out on the veranda. On the terrace were picnic tables in the sun where guests could bring their lunch and have wine with it.

All around the estate acres of vineyards lay carefully tended. Grapevines climbed support railings and wound around the strings tied between. Row after row they leaned carefully in the heat of the sun. The view of the vineyards and the lake and mountains beyond was suddenly not real. David forgot we were in Canada. "You see," I said. "You do not have to go to the French Riviera. Everything is right here."

I could not get him away from the veranda where he stood glued to the view. I went in and joined a group that had been set up for wine tasting. In little glasses the proprietor poured a dash of every type of wine the winery produced. We tasted them all. For the next round I went out and dragged David up to the bar. He tasted all the wines. All the wines with French names. He did not say a word. Every mouthful was swirled about as he appeared intellectually engaged, ignoring everything else. At the end he bought three bottles of some kind of Chardonnay.

We came away from the estate with heads buzzing. The sunshine was sweeter than before, the green was softer than before and the blue of the sky was hazier. David took a last look over the vineyards.

"I want to be a vintner," he declared. "I want to produce exclusive estate wines."
"Are you sure?" I interrupted. "Isn't Canadian publishing a good enough occupation?"
"I'm positive of it," he assured.
He did not say much after that. He was thinking. He said Canadian wines were good after all. He had not known they were so good.

ELEVEN

BUT WHY WOULD I FORGET? WHY WOULD I WANT TO FORGET?
It would be so useless, so lifeless, not to treasure everything I remember, every moment I spent, even with a
stranger. Because some people are close to you even
when they are not. There are people whose every
movement you are aware of. You do not know why you
are so aware of them but you are. When he looks down
or up, when he listens, when he does not. When he
walks away, rounds a corner, disappears from sight,
you follow all his movements even when you are not
following them. No one there could say you are following someone's movements but you are. Not with
your eyes. You see with your skin, your hair, your ears.
You see with all your senses. When he comes and sits
down beside you, you do not have to look up. You

know it is him. You have waited for him to sit beside you but you did not know you were waiting for him. It seems like an accident. He did not know you had noticed but you did. You were waiting for him and you did not know you were expecting him. You begin to sense he is aware of you. He follows your movements with his eyes and ears. His skin is aware of you, his fingers folded under his elbow are aware of you. Some people are close in spite of all efforts not be. Why should you deny that? There must be a reason. A chemical reason, a biological reason, a spiritual reason. It could even be a religious reason. A writerly reason, readerly reason. I wanted to know if Jules was a Catholic.

"Are you a Catholic?"

"No."

"What are you?"

"Nothing. I was a Catholic once but now I am nothing.

"What are you?"

"Nothing."

"Nothing?"

"I was not a Lutheran once and now I am a nothing."

"I saw a picture of Luther when I was a boy in Catholic school. He was, how do you say...?" He raised his shoulders and made a stern face. The face of a grim schoolmaster.

"They would not give you a nice image of Luther in Catholic school."

"No. Is there a nice image of Luther?"

"The Danish Luther is nice."

"How is that?"

"Not grim."

"Do they believe in sin?"

"Yes. It is a sin not to enjoy life."

"Oh, it is the biggest sin."

"You think?"

"Oh, yes."

The morning light was crawling in the window on all fours, damaged by the sudden return of winter overnight. Why would I want to forget the return of winter? It is not fitting that winter should return just then. That people with wildly different spiritual backgrounds should wake up one morning in perfect spiritual agreement. But nothing should fit, nothing is right. All the lectures and scoldings and reprimands poured on the heads of the very young wash off like the baptismal water and are dry before anyone has become aware of them. Under all our differences we are exactly alike. We are mirror images of one another. We follow each other's movements as though they were our own. We are learning with our senses. With our skin, our fingers, our tongues, we are learning to be in perfect spiritual agreement. I do not want to forget we agreed that we cannot regret what we do. We choose to remember. He gave me words. A text. A language not my own. It is a gift I can keep and it will be mine forever and he does not know he gave me this gift. If I tell him what he brought he will be surprised. He did not bring flowers. He was apologetic. But there was a gift and he knew there was a gift. The gift was in his hand. It was lying inside the palm of his hand. When he opened his hand I could feel it there.

TWELVE

PERHAPS WE ALREADY RECOGNIZED THAT A MILLION SIGNIFI-
cant perceptions had passed in the air. That we define
ourselves in terms of each other. That we cannot exist
in a monologue. Yet our dialogue is without words.
There is no official agreement, no absolute truth. It is
only an outdated morality that says I cannot desire
whomever I want. The morality of a world I never saw
and never lived in. A remnant of a past my forefathers
have told me about but of no concern to me. In this
world there is no morality. No truth about human
actions. The only truth I find is what is not expected.
Not accepted. Not officially correct. My mistakes are
the most significant thing about me. My mistakes
define me. What I cannot say defines me. What I cannot say to him because he cannot hear defines me. I

have known him for a long time and this is our first meeting. What was it that passed in the air before? For this reason perhaps we lagged behind. We were going from one place to another. It is immaterial where we were going except we had to go. It is immaterial who was with us. People. Several people walking ahead of us, going to an elevator to be lifted up. We must have been in the bowels of an institution, deep below ground in the caverns of a building. Jules made us lag behind until all the people had rounded the corners ahead of us and we were alone. He was laughing and I was laughing and I no longer remember why. There is a point at which the interstated dialogue becomes an official story. A point at which others can recognize that something of significance has happened. That is where Jules becomes another. He becomes a man in a green coat whose arm was around me. The man was laughing at something. He was pulling me back so the others would disappear. His arm was around me and he stopped to pull me toward him and he kissed me. He had never kissed me before. There was no reason for it. Then he looked at me as if he had surprised himself. Just as though a blue haze had materialized from the floor and the genie had swung out of Aladdin's lamp. Something extraordinary. Something said without words. A kiss. But a kiss is significant. It tells an official story. It is something identifiable to others. It is where we agreed. It is so much easier now to talk about desire. Perhaps it is just his presence, one spirit desiring another, one language desiring the presence of another. Bilingualism. My English desires his French. It is that simple. Without the other language my words have no significance. His mouth on mine. A meeting of languages. Unofficial bilingualism. We are defined by our desires, by what we want. *What does English Canada want?* No one asked the question but it was in the air. English Canada wants the presence of French Canada. It wants to swirl French words in its mouth like good wine, to taste the words in French. It wants the arm of a handsome man around its shoulder. *What does French Canada want?* A kiss. A stolen kiss and separation.

THIRTEEN

THE DANCE OF APPROACH AND REJECTION IS STILLED IN THE Okanagan Valley. In the early morning only a mild haze penetrates the air. The water is almost blank. Sometimes the sun that just creeps over the hill shines a mellow band onto the incandescent water. Then ripples can be seen. A tiny breaking of the surface, a ruffling of the tranquility of dawn.

It is a landscape that requires no stance, no answers. No position, no preparations. A landscape that couches those of us who live here in mellow arms and asks nothing of us. A gentle mother who allows us to rest awhile. We can rest just by looking at the hazy green morning of early spring. When all is awakening.

·

What is a sentence that is at rest? Could I write a sentence that has no tension in it? No elliptical curve from desire to return? A sentence that acknowledges it is tired and wants to rest. The sentence knows what it wants. To rest awhile. A sentence without an Other. Without a lover. Without a desired object. Perhaps even a sentence without a subject. No ego. No narcissistic ego settling its image over the world.

·

I came to this valley because I wanted all that tension to seep out of the phrases all around me. To uncharge the battery of my language. I was tired. The words were crammed too full. They could not hold the wealth of information and counterinformation I had put there. They were so full that it was impossible to recognize what was in them. I wanted to see the disappointments that had accrued fall like fluff from the branches. To see the naked branches.

·

As the morning lingers the haze melts away. I see the water more clearly. It is blank. There is no wind. The pastures and orchards are reflected in the lake. The sun is behind a thin cloud and the air is soft. So soft. It has the sheen of silk and the texture of cotton.

FOURTEEN

DAVID STEERED THE BOAT WITH HIS FEET. HE SAT ON THE upper deck in the sun. In one hand he held a can of beer. In the other hand a perpetual cigarette. The boat was crawling forward at eight miles per hour. When another boat went by, the waves created a rocking motion. I lay on the roof of the houseboat, sunbathing. My eyes were closed. The sun was warm and I was melting in the comfort of yellow summer and blue air. The low drone of the boat engine barely reached my ears.

"We still have a job to do," I heard him say from the deck.
"What's that?" I answered blearily from the roof.
"We have to find a title for your book."
"I'll think about it."

"Think hard. How does *Relative Distance* strike you?"

"How about *Point de capiton*," I said in half dream.

"No."

"*La où c'était.*"

"No."

"*Moments féconds.*"

"No."

I opened my eyes and watched the mountainside glide by slowly. The peaks towered in the distance. The mountain was covered in pine forest. Green and thick, the trees covered the slopes. Then as suddenly as thunder there was a bald patch. A naked area where clear-cutting had taken place. All along the shorelines of the Shuswap Lakes patches of clear-cutting dotted the mountainsides and were alarmingly large and frequent. They were empty areas. Areas made naked for paper. For houses. For pulp.

On the beaches people swam. Children jumped and screamed. Adults lingered slowly, reclining on mattresses, resting in inner tubes. I thought a landscape is like a language. The reason I like to live here is simple. Because this is where people come when they make holes in their lives. Naked patches in busy routines. Holes they can escape through. Inside the life emptied of routine and obligations I hear them laughing. The lake shore rings with the laughter of those who have escaped their lives.

I like best the ellipsis in the sentence. The gap in the construction. The alarming hesitation. It is so dark in the cracked juncture of my sentence. It is a black hole. An area made naked.

FIFTEEN

"I WISH I HAD KISSED YOU ON THE RAILROAD TRACK," JULES SAID.

"Were you thinking of it?"

"Yes."

We had found an escape. A space in our wildly different lives that somehow made room for us both. Like water that parts when you enter and closes behind you when you depart, this space would fill in again when we were gone. No trace of us would exist. No one coming after us would be able to identify our presence. No one would know where we were. In this alternate space, a double of reality, a negative of reality, things became disproportionately significant. His hands. His lips. The ability to forget. To forget who you are and where you have been and where you are going. To forget that you were ever alone on the mountainside, alone with the ponderosas. That you ever wept because someone corrected you all the time. That you were ever confused because someone redefined you and you no longer recognized yourself. That you were dismissed or rejected or lost. To forget that anything ever happened. Instead his arms, his whole body. A space of pure affection. Nothing but affection that fills the room like water. Every corner, every crack in this space is filled with affection. A soft gentle affection, like the early spring air in the valley, when it is made of cotton, of silk, of incandescence. A laying on of hands. A blessing that says forget. The embrace of a stranger who is no longer a stranger because you have known him a long time. His arms are strong and you can feel the presence of something wildly different. Another world. He carries another world with him like a haze. In his presence you can feel the existence of another world and you are happy. You are glad the world you inhabit is not the only one. If it were the only world you would be dismayed. You would be closed in and unable to get out. But in his arms you remember there are other worlds. It will be much easier now to take my bags to the airport. To fly to another city. To see my bags come out the trapdoor at the airport in another world. There people speak another language. You are so happy to hear another language, to remember you once had another language yourself. A language you had almost forgotten. You recognize you have spent too long with people who think their world is the only world. They have all been solipsistic and you have been listening to one side of a conversation for too long. You recognize you have been living in a place of nothing but Mussolinis and Stalins and Hitlers and you are so tired of dictators. You are so weary of tyrants. They made you weep and your weeping was antisocial and you went away into the mountains just to stop the tears. Jules does not know the gift he has brought. The blessing of his hands that says yes. Yes. There is another world. There are many other worlds. It will be so much easier to travel now. He was speaking another language. It was French. The air of Montréal. The air of Paris. Your own cities are suddenly visible in the light he sheds. Copenhagen, Oslo, Stockholm. Cities whose air you carry with you, an air that makes you antisocial. That makes dictators want to correct you. That drives tyrants to redefine you in terms of a world you do not belong in and the definition is all wrong and you cannot fix it again. But in this space you can feel there are other worlds. Worlds that are gentle. Whose touch is soft as a whisper. The whisper of a barely discernible breeze on an island. The grasses waver so gently there. The highland flowers shudder so imperceptibly there.

SIXTEEN

ONE MORNING WHEN I LOOKED OUT THE KITCHEN WINDOW I saw that my biggest apricot tree had fallen. It was the tree just outside the window, the one I enjoyed looking at when I put water on for coffee. Now it lay on the ground, spread across the hillside that made up my front yard. It had fallen over all the juniper bushes growing to keep the soil from eroding and moving down to the cottage. It must have been the fruit. The branches had grown so heavy with fruit that the whole tree fell with a crack and lay spread out on my property.

I called Josef the yardkeeper. He came and sawed the tree into bits of firewood and stacked them in the woodpile behind the cottage. Nothing remained but the broken stump of a formerly magnificent tree laden with golden fruit.

For better or for worse this is where I live. I live in the ellipsis. The break in a continuum. The crack in a line. The juncture in a phrase. The hole in a life. The breathing space. The breathing space they sometimes call a tourist trap. The place we would like to be trapped in but never have time. The vacation spot. The carnival where Ferris wheels roll and whistles blow and laughter can be heard ringing among the bells.

I did not think large trees fell down like that. I thought they were strong and sturdy. I did not think the joy of living would fell them. Because the moments had been too fruitful the apricot tree fell of its own weight. Something about this tree on the ground struck me as absurd. So absurd I laughed.

SEVENTEEN

PERHAPS EVERYTHING I HAVE BEEN THINKING RUNS INTO pain. Pain and loss. I have been thinking about the early morning sun that beams into my cottage. The silver sheen it casts on the lake. The woods above drowsy in the first notes of forest birds. I have been thinking that under the clouds I have lost my mirror. All surfaces become opaque. I can no longer see myself. I am reflected in nothing. No face looks back at me in recognition. All faces are strangers. I have no memory of my origins. There are only strange American towns. We witness the return of winter in the new daylight. We thought it was spring. We left our coats behind and walked in the spring air. It was warm and the sun shone. But I do not recognize anything I see. Perhaps all stories run into chaos. No matter how well constructed, how well organized, all stories end in chaos. In disaster. Life itself ends in disaster. We are riding the rails of the dead end. The train will have no brakes. The tracks will continue until they stop and there will be no warning of their ending. They might stop at the edge of a cliff. The story will be a cliff-hanger. The train will go over the cliff at full speed. All the cars will disassemble in flight. The ground below will be littered with train wreckage. Attempts at body counts will be made. But the bodies will no longer be recognizable. Identities cannot be certified. Relatives will be warned against visiting the site. Ropes will be strung around the wreckage. Officials will look bewildered. They will claim ignorance. *We did not know it ended there. How could we know the tracks were like that?*

There are no signs. NO THRU ROAD. If there are signs they tell us nothing. We wonder what they mean. A sign that says LAST CHANCE FRUIT STAND. But there is no fruit stand. It is winter. The shacks by the road are boarded up. No fresh fruit arrives in winter. The sign itself is bent over and has been in the rain too long. The painted words are blurred. A sign that says NO U TURN. But there is no You to turn to. Nothing to forbid. Nothing to warn about. No consequences. Only the mellow drops of rain.

It has been raining all along. The early spring rain is made of satin. It is the evening gown of the beautiful earth. She thinks there will be fruitful moments in the early evening. But there are no fruitful moments, only a light rain falling. The drops have brought down the lightest cloud cover. The clouds drift down the hillside. They penetrate between the trees. All runs into chaos. The sky, the clouds, the woods, the water. Soon they will be indistinguishable. I will be unable to tell them apart. There will be rain on my hands. My hair. My arms and face. I will be unable to see where the tracks are going or whether a train is coming or not. The bright light in front will not be visible until it is too late.

EIGHTEEN

FIRST ONLY AN OCCASIONAL ONE APPEARED OUT OF
nowhere. It would sit on the cottage wall outside without movement. A large brown insect, larger than a bee
and smaller than a bat. It would be impossible to tell
where it came from. The creature would crawl very
slowly, with difficulty, toward some indefinite goal. It
would be easy to smash with a shoe but if attacked it
would emit a strong unpleasant odor. Something less
incisive than the smell of a skunk but equally distasteful.
The cats would refuse to touch it.

Then there were more of them. They crawled across
the veranda like languid potatoes. They slithered up the
walls. They sat on the steps as if stunned. Only occa-
sionally did one of them fly. It took an extraordinary

event to make them fly but when in the air they flew rapidly.

People in the valley called them stink bugs. Some said seeder bugs. The radio broadcast discussions on the infestation of the Rocky Mountain Pine Bark Beetle. The neighbors said the beetles came every fall, sometimes in droves. They soon littered the outside walls of the cottage. When the door was opened they crawled inside or flew through the doorway. Even when no doors or windows were opened the bugs came inside. It was impossible to tell how they found their way indoors.

The neighbors said the bugs like it inside when the sun is too hot. In the heat of the day the stink bugs could not be seen. They hid in the wood, in cracks and grooves of wooden railings and cottage siding. Then in the evening they crawled out again. Sometimes a bug would fall down, apparently from nowhere. Perhaps from flying or a belabored attempt at crossing from one point to another. A bug would crash with the low humming of an engine gone berserk and out of control. The stink bugs malfunctioned easily. They were too heavy for themselves. They crashed in strange sites. They would crash onto the table on the veranda and lie dazed next to a glass of iced tea. They crashed into the hair of someone bending down to pick a weed. They crashed next to the face of someone lying on a mat sunbathing.

They were the clumsiest bugs ever invented. Yet no matter how clumsy they were their numbers continued to increase.

People said the beetles would disappear when the weather turned cold. But the weather turned cold and the bugs were still there. Snow fell and they crawled out from under snowbanks. Frost came and they crawled in and out of cracks in the wood anyway. They would not stop. They never stopped.

NINETEEN

IN THE SPRING, WHEN I FIRST CAME TO THE VALLEY TO BUY A cottage to live in, there were floods. Rain had been falling for weeks. The lakes rose and overflowed their shorelines. Water rolled over the highway. The floating bridge between Kelowna and Westbank was under water. Backyards that faced the water shrank. Some houses flooded.

The hills in the valley are sandy and loose. It is not a rainy country. Unlike the West Coast, the Okanagan Valley sees more heat than water and forests struggle against the odds to stay alive in the dry soil. The hills are barren in places. The mountainsides are parched dry. They glower back at the hot sun in their naked-ness. If it suddenly rains too much there is no vegetation to keep the soil together. The hills erode. There are mud avalanches.

When the floodrains fell, avalanches occurred. Houses began to move in the transferral of mud. Trailers sailed down the hill. Houses bent over and cracked. Some houses collapsed entirely. What was left of houses washed away in the rush of water falling downhill. A family sat down to supper and between the salad and chicken stew, the house came down. A mudslide fell from the mountain behind it and landed on the roof of the house.

The Premier of British Columbia came in a helicopter to investigate the damage. He looked at washed-away roads, fallen road signs, collapsed walls. He was seen peering over the edge of a cliff at some wooden rubble in the bottom of a canyon. "Is that someone's home too?" he was heard saying.

But my cottage on the hillside was dry. Forests of jack pines and ponderosa pines were all around it. There was no way for the mountains to move just from a falling rain. From my dry cottage I could watch the disasters below. How some people's lives were running into chaos. I could think about the beautiful rain coming like silver from the sky. How it brings down the clouds. How all things are stirred.

TWENTY

JULES AND I WERE WALKING ON BACKROADS AT THE EDGE OF
that midwestern American town. We did not know
where the road led but we followed it out of town. Soon
fields were all around us. Fields of early spring, not yet
ready for planting. There was almost no snow left on
the landscape. A grain elevator broke the continuum of
flatness. A railroad track traversed the land, cutting
through roads and fields with a dominance all its own.
"Let's walk on the railroad track," Jules suggested. We
went up to the track and followed it into the country.
Soon nothing was around us. Our only signpost was the
track. He was telling me stories. A story about two men
in Québec. They were friends. They were famous
friends and they walked on the railroad track together.
A train came and they would not leave the tracks. They

let themselves be mowed down by the train. Perhaps they did not hear the whistle blow. Perhaps they wanted it that way, to be plowed down together. A final act. A final friendship. I said I knew of only one such incident. A boy walking alone on the tracks in Manitoba. He did not hear the train coming because he had a Walkman on his ears. Fog hung over the fields where we walked, a haze that colored all things blue. We could not see into the distance very far. All sound was muffled. The wind was blowing when we got to the open fields. We could feel the wind seeping into our hair, our jackets, our fingers. Jules turned the collar of his coat up. We were telling stories, two solitudes. He speculated that the two friends wanted it that way. It was impossible that they did not hear the train. Something must have happened. There must have been a break in their friendship. In their lives. A break just large enough for a train to plow into it. I thought of the story of Elvira Madigan. A man and a woman are in love. They are a carnival woman and a soldier. She is beautiful and has flowing red hair. They cannot have each other. It is forbidden. They run away into the woods together and no one knows where they are. They lie on the ground together. They tell stories to each other while they eat the berries in the woods and drink from the spring. He has a gun on his belt and he shoots the woman. Then he shoots himself. They are gone, just like that. A cold wind was blowing over the American Midwest. Jules turned his collar up and his dark-haired profile faced the wind. We walked slowly because there was nowhere to go to. Loose spikes lay on the tracks, unearthed by the violence of passing trains. There were no people, no cars, no birds, no life. The landscape was empty. Only the two of us. I was thinking I wanted nothing after this. To walk on these tracks endlessly. To follow the wooden bars and spikes as far as they went. This was a break in the continuum of our lives. Unplanned, unofficial. We had escaped and no one knew where we were. He said he was a press clipper for NATO once. He cut out of newspapers articles of interest. I was thinking it must be necessary to know more than one language. If you know only one language you cannot tell which articles are of interest. There was no sound anywhere. His voice telling stories was the only sound and it broke the silence like the tearing of a sheet or the ripping of a curtain. Something that let the bleak daylight into the world. The overcast sky and the cold wind. There was nothing to hear. I was looking out to the horizon. My eyes were following the tracks. In the distance I saw a bright light emerging from the haze. It must be the light of a train approaching.

"I think a train is coming," I warned.

"No, I do not think it is a train." He did not see the train. We walked on.

"If it is a train," I whispered, "it will mow us down."

"Yes."

We would perish together. Like the two friends. There

would be press clippings. *Two Canadians perish on railroad tracks.* They had broken away. They were taking a walk and a train unexpectedly crushed them. The train seemed to come from nowhere. The engine was out of control and the loud humming burst across the fields. Perhaps they did it on purpose. It is impossible that they did not hear the train. There would be speculation. We were walking slowly because there was nowhere to get to. In the distance a bright light was blasting out of the fog. There was no sound. The light ripped through the haze. Then he saw the headlight coming at us. "It looks like a train after all," he agreed. We stepped off the tracks and stood watching as the train sped by. It was a quiet train. Only a low humming of the engine as it passed. There were many cars. Boxcars. The boxcars had words written on them. They said PILLSBURY. "Pillsbury," he read out loud. "The train is full of cookies!" I was thinking if we had not left the tracks we would have been plowed down by a train full of cookies. There would be strange clippings. *Two solitudes perish under American cookie train.*

TWENTY-ONE

JULES WAS SLEEPING. THE LIGHT OF A STREETLAMP OUTSIDE shone into the dark room through a crack in the curtains. He did not notice the blaring light. Through the crack I could see new snow flurries outside. I was thinking of the other lives. Lives we could have led but did not choose. Choices we did not make. The alternate paths. That what we choose is real only because we choose it. Perhaps what we have not chosen is even more real. Perhaps those lives are being led anyway in some other realm. There are official stories and then there are unofficial stories. Sometimes we break through the official story. We escape into an alternate story. Just for a while. A day, a night. Two days, three. Four nights. However long. We taste the possibilities of other lives. Other stories. We roll them in our mouths like good wine. No one knows where we are. We have dropped out of the picture and we cannot be found. We live behind the scenes for a while. Others are calling from the stage. The audience is waiting. Expectations hang in the air. Two presences are missing. The stage setting is incomplete. Two chairs are empty. Someone is calling and we do not hear. I come into the room late. Hundreds of people are there. They are dressed in nice clothes. They have just put down their wine glasses and are seated in rows. They are smiling. I am late and I greet them as elegantly as I can in my wet shoes and paltry clothing. I have just come in from the snow. I have been walking along a track through the woods and it has been getting dark. I think I am lost but then I see the towering building. I am glad to be inside and find all the people in the large room. There is a stage and a few people sit in chairs on the stage. One chair is empty. I realize it is my chair. I try to hurry so I will not be late but my shoes are heavy. I make belabored attempts at walking to the stage. I see their faces waiting. Jules is already there. He is in his chair. He has come indoors ahead of me. Somehow he has managed to get there in time. I go up the stairs to the stage and it seems as if I am crawling. I wonder if they notice I am crawling. If I go too fast I might fall. My chair is standing there alone. Empty. Then Jules was awake and he held me. I buried my face in his chest. I did not want to see the light of the streetlamp blasting in on us. The light was coming closer and closer and I did not want to look.

TWENTY-TWO

ALL THE THINGS WE DO NOT SAY ARE FILED AWAY SOME-
where in another realm. Way back in our distant memories. Only we know about them. When we dream they
crawl out of the cracks and remind us that we might
have said something. We might have done something.
Our lives might have turned out differently. If he had
kissed me on the railroad track we would have forgotten
ourselves in the moment. We would not have heard the
train rolling out of the fog. We would not have seen the
headlights. The train would have mowed us down at
that moment. It might have been the kiss of death.
Instead we sat at a table and Jules told stories that made
me laugh. I could not stop laughing. Perhaps it was the
laughter of relief. A narrow escape. The cliff-hanger.

TWENTY-THREE

ROBERTA AND JUSTINE HAD PICKED SO MANY APRICOTS THAT I invited them for a reward. I told them that for their harvesting work they would be taken for a sailing trip on a paddle wheeler. Justine was touristing from Cologne. To go on a paddle-wheel boat on Okanagan Lake she came out in her cotton summer skirt and blouse with a small sweater hanging on her arm. She was smiling.

I drove them to town and down to the docks where a paddle wheeler lay. People were boarding. The heat of the summer day was still in the air. We went on board. This boat, we were told, used to paddle the lake from end to end. It would carry things from Penticton to Kelowna and back. Then a floating bridge was built across the lake and the boat could not get through. Suddenly there were roads. Highways were built and it became faster to take a load by truck. Now the boat paddles in circles for tourists. It is without direction. Lost in the circles of its own circumference.

There was a buffet of food. Music was playing and people were dancing. We watched the paddle wheel plow the waters, throwing up streams of the lake as it emerged from the depths. It was a festive boat. We began to tour the lake, skirting the edges of the large shoreline. Dusk fell as we watched the hazy green landscape turn maroon in the falling light. After the dinner we walked on the upper deck. All the people came to the upper deck with glasses in their hands and smiles on their faces.

Roberta and Justine were engaged in happy conversation. They marveled at the lake. They criticized the music. They spoke of memories and laughed at possibilities. I was looking at the increasingly dark water where it parted as the boat furrowed its way forward. Where it gathered behind us as if we had not been there. Only a few remaining ripples signaled that we had plowed our way across. On the hillsides houses were built scenically. Lush gardens surrounded the houses.

I was thinking it is so simple to be happy. It should be

so simple yet it is not. Remnants of outdistanced poems went through my mind. *There hath passed a glory from the earth*. Yet it was impossible to tell what the glory was. Where it came from. Where it went to. Whether it might not still be here, hiding, undetected. Showing itself only at certain moments. The moment complete darkness has set in. When the water is black and nothing but darkness can be seen where the hills and mountains were before. And in the darkness, lights glow. The festive lights of town as we sail into harbor again. Strings of light beaded around the dock. They are like golden drops in a sea of darkness. Golden moments.

TWENTY-FOUR

THE BEDROOM OF MY COTTAGE IN THE VALLEY HAS LARGE French doors leading to the veranda overlooking the lake. From there I can see the moonlight on the water. I lie down in the bed and see a broad band of silver glowing across the water. The moon is large and full. It is pale as a giant pearl in the night sky. I can see how fog rolls in at night, how the air thickens.

.

I find myself caught on the edges of irresolution. Between happiness and sadness. Confidence and fear. All emotions roll together. Happy memories and unhappy ones. Caught in an inability to distinguish one from the other. The happy moments are the most dangerous. They are dangerous because you want them.

You desire what you must not have. You desire your own ruin. *What he desires presents itself to him as what he does not want*, Jacques Lacan said. The permanence of his desire transmitted to an intermittent ego. This way I can pretend that my desire is intermittent. It is a fleeting desire. I do not know what I want.

.

I would say I am tired. I love the rain. The rain has been falling all night. In the early dawn the wood of my veranda is wet. The branches of the pine trees are wet. The juniper bushes are wet. I love the clouds sleeping between the hills. The clouds were so tired. They lowered themselves into the valley between the hills and went to sleep. They are laden with rain. They are full of sorrow. They are too heavy for themselves.

TWENTY-FIVE

JUST AS SUDDENLY THE MORNING IS BRILLIANT AND BRIGHT.
The sun casts a yellow glow over everything. The pastures are jewel green. The forests are majestic, stretch-
ing into the air as if newly awoken. The roofs of barns
glow with reflections of light. Shadows fall across open
spaces languorously. A solitary boat appears on the lake
and meanders its way across the water. A hawk glides
smoothly above the trees.

I realize the winter is departing. The cold clouds that
covered the valley for many months have lifted and let
the sunlight in. I know there will be blossoms any day
now. All the world awakens as if from a difficult dream.
An unresolvable dream where questions remained
unanswered. Where no hope had a foothold. Where

faces were tense. It is much easier to be happy now. It occurs to me that being alive to see the brilliant spring morning arrive is enough. Just to be able to tell the story that spring is rounding the corner.

.

My friend Roger lives in the valley in the British Columbia interior. He lives in a cottage among the trees across the lake from me. I had forgotten I had a friend across the lake. Perhaps it is the arrival of spring that reminds me.

When it was winter Roger slid down the ice to my cottage. He brought bottles of good wine. They were experiments, he said. We tasted different vintages, rolling the wine in our mouths. He told stories that made me laugh. About being stoned and listening to Earl Birney read poems. Watching the poet's ego rise from him in a blue cloud and fill the room with a purple haze. I was cooking, squeezing lemon juice over pieces of chicken. The frost outside was deep. Ice clung to the fenceposts with a frantic grip.

In the winter Roger brought a pot of yellow flowers to brighten up my cottage. I neglected the flowers. I forget to give them water. The yellow heads drooped and the green leaves withered because I had forgotten my friend. Perhaps my mind was elsewhere. Perhaps I was of two minds.

When it was first spring we remembered we were friends. We were such good friends that when we crossed the street in Vernon strangers called after us *Newlyweds!* Because we could not stop kissing each other. Because in spring in the valley all things are kissing. The bees kiss each other, the birds, the cats and dogs, the first purple flowers. The trees in the orchard before the blossoms come. The trees reach out their bare arms and beg each other for the last embraces of winter.

.

Roger said, "I gotta do a lot of thinking." He had more than one woman. He was overextended.
I said, "Like unto like. I have more than one man."

I came to this valley so I would not have any man. Just to have the golden ripples jittering across the deep maroon water of the lake below my cottage. Just to see the slow rowboat paddling over. Just to be happy there is such a thing as life. Life without belonging, without ownership. Life with memories in it, like unopened buds on trees in the orchard. I know that when spring comes the buds will open and there will be blossoms. Insects will come and kiss the blossoms. There will be fruit hanging from the branches. Heavy fruit laden with gold.

TWENTY-SIX

IT OCCURS TO ME I HAVE BEEN DREAMING. THAT JULES' windblown face is a dream. His dark hair ruffled by the chilly winter wind. His collar turned up against the cold. Press clippings flying all over the railroad tracks. Cookies falling out of boxcars and crumbling in the last bit of snow on the ground. A dream we both awoke from. It was a new day. The palm of his hand lay across his forehead. He awoke in a large bed with pillows and sheets. There was an opening between the curtains where the bright light blasted in. He was thinking, his elbow in the air and his hand on his forehead.

"Where are you?" I asked and could barely hear myself asking.

"Have you heard of cloud nine?"

"Yes."

"I am on cloud twelve. Cloud fourteen."

All the clouds were rising. It was easy to see the clouds lift lightly into the air. One by one they rose from the sleeping valley. From between the hills where their own weight had pulled them down. The sun was beaming on them and the water that was in them was dissipating. Their sorrow was vanishing. As they grew lighter they floated up. Behind them was blue sky, so azure it was like a gem. The clouds floated into the sky, becoming whiter and lighter as they did so. They were flying home. I could no longer count the clouds, there were so many. But when I looked out the window I saw the angry snow and I knew we were not dreaming. That rising from this bed would be the beginning of a distance. An immense distance we would be unable to close again. Wildly different lives waited to greet us at the ends of that opening. A difference of French and English. Of city and country. A distance of mountains, lakes, rivers, fields, pastures, suburbs. Everything that lay across the country would lie between us. Time itself would lie between us. We would forget each other. Time would place our images in a dream. It is a dream you did not know you had. I was thinking that even though his arms are around me and his body is around me I can feel the unbridgeable gap. The separation is in the moment even while the moment is expanding to contain all time in it. The waters are rushing to the edges of the lake. The lake is rising and overflowing its boundaries. The floating bridge is under water. It is impossible to travel across.

TWENTY-SEVEN

HOW QUICKLY THE CLOUDS DISSIPATE. WHEN I ARISE IN THE
early morning we are enveloped in thick cloud and fog.
It is as though we have been moving during our sleep
from our comfortable beds with many duvets and cush-
ions billowing about us into an ethereal sphere high
above the earth. A place of nothing but cloud. When I
look out the window I can see nothing at all. There is
only a thick gray substance, as if the whole cottage had
been placed inside the center of the fog.

Then the day advances and the fog begins to separate.
The thick haze over the lake remains, cradling the
water. Above, the mist releases itself and turns into bil-
lowy white clouds. The fluffy bundles start floating up
and between them and the lake the image of mountain-

sides appears. Soon I can make out the slanting hill-sides, the open pastures, the forest. There is still a bit of snow on top of the mountains. Between the trees I can see layers of white dust.

The mist over the lake itself begins to rise. Underneath I see how the water is perfectly blank. In its face I see reflected the rising clouds. The water appears like a giant layer of marble. I know if I went down there and looked in the blank surface of the lake I would see my face clearly. I do not know if it would be the face of a stranger.

It has been raining all night. I could hear the heavy drops falling in the eavestroughs and on the roof. The rain fell straight down because there was no wind. There was just the sheer force of gravity bringing down the water in the clouds. In the morning puddles lie still on the porch. The front steps are wet. Huge drops still hang from the roof, uncertain about letting go. The grass holds up beads of rainwater for the sun to see.

I put on my coat and boots and walk up the wet gravel of the road. The path from my cottage goes through the forest. The forest on such mornings is somber. The overcast sky keeps the pine trees dark and moody. In the hills above, the trees appear to be waiting for the sun. Like all the world they wait for the warmth of sunshine. I like to walk among the ponderosa pines. Everywhere the gentle ponderosas stand with tufts of needles on their branches.

There was a sudden blast of wind in the night. It came and went so quickly that it was hardly detectable. But it was so strong it tore objects from their places. When I come up on the road I see that a giant jack pine has been ripped out of the earth by the wind. The trunk lies across the road in complete defeat. The branches have splintered off in the violence of the impact. Bits of branches lie everywhere. When I look at the earth where the tree was uprooted I see the roots spreading dizzyingly into the air. I can tell how shallow the roots were. I see it is no wonder the tree fell down. Perhaps this sandy soil is hostile to such trees. Perhaps the whole forest is tottering on the brink of collapse, the tiny root systems just barely holding the heavy trunks steady.

I cannot help wondering if it is so hard to find a foothold in the West. Not even the native trees can do it. A little blast of wind is all it takes. Perhaps this is not true. Perhaps this is not true at all.

TWENTY-EIGHT

THESE MIDWESTERN AMERICAN TOWNS ARE SO THIN AND
lonely. They lie in a landscape where you can walk in
one direction until you perish. Nothing breaks the
monotony of the flat plain and sky. In the early spring
trucks kick up dust on the highway. They round the
corner as the road bends and leave a cloud of dust to
settle on the wayside. Jules came to walk with me into
the prairie, on the railroad tracks, and I was happy he
did. Because we always know who people are long
before we know them. That he should be walking
beside me in the emptiness of the prairie was unfitting.
But nothing should fit. He carried his cities with him
but they dissipated in the afternoon air. I was thinking *I
remember Montréal.* Coming down Sherbrooke on just
this kind of day. Early spring, before winter has depart-

ed and summer has begun. The snow piled thick on the streets and sidewalks had begun to melt. Everywhere the slush lay in massive half-crystalline puddles turned brown by passing traffic. I had to stop in a store and buy rubber boots. It was a dingy store that sold cheap things across from the college. I paid for the boots and put them on at the counter. Then I went out again and stepped in the puddles. It was a bright day. Before I got home I stopped in a café. I was gathering my mind. I did not want to be home on the West side just yet. Where the dog was and the lace curtains and the heavy furniture that came from another era. Where I knocked and entered at the same time, unsure of which to do first. Where I was always knocking in some sense or other, not of the family, not out of it. Neither here nor there. Where the woman I thought of as my mother-in-law was making soup in a pot in the kitchen. It was chicken soup seasoned with chicken bouillon. Where the photographs were, snapshots of lives I did not recognize. Lives I memorized like a foreign language. With a dictionary and a phrase book. I read words in another language in my bed at night. I listened to *Radio Canada. Ici Radio Canada.* Thinking it was an irony that the language of my own country should be foreign to me. I practiced my French on the waitress who brought me café au lait on that cold afternoon. I read the *Gazette*, making time tick forward as I watched the snow turn to slush. My feet were dry in my new rubber boots. I was memorizing the lives of Montréal. People who fought with their fists. Who refused to speak English. I said to my sister-in-law: "Why not learn to speak English?" But she said, "No. No more languages, please." And I eventually left the bistro and rounded the corner to the house. The brick houses stood all in a row. But here in the American Midwest, there it is here again. That particular Montréal. And I remember other Montréals. The theater where people in costumes sang with high-pitched voices. Where pieces of fruit went into warm chocolate pots. Where dark alleys left you without direction. Dimly lit restaurants whose names were outside the door. Masses of people strolled downtown at night without destination. I remember dancing. Remember listening to strange sounds from a microphone. Remember laughing. Stolen kisses. And it always seemed everything happened at the same time in Montréal. But here in the American Midwest things happen one at a time. One after the other, one step ahead of the other. A chronological progression that somehow seems unnatural. Jules was with me and he was talking and I was thinking it was unnatural that all things should not be happening at once here too. Everything I imagined in the past and will imagine in the future. That it should all be happening as we stepped from tie to tie on the track.

"Do you have a technique for walking on the tracks?" he asked, bemused.

"No."

I had no technique for anything. I do not think there

will be enough repetitions to develop a technique. There are only circles and every circle strikes you as new. You do not remember having done this before. I looked at Jules' windblown profile and did not remember having done this before. Just precisely this. I was thinking it is not possible that this combination will ever crystallize again either. It is a solitary moment. All alone in its immensity.

TWENTY-NINE

I HAVE A COTTAGE IN THE COUNTRY. IN THE COUNTRY WHAT-
ever happens, happens in nature. When snow falls.
When fog sets in. When trees fall down across the road.
When the lake freezes. When it is picking season. The
only carnivals here are nature's own. The only festivals,
the only holidays, are supplied by the hills and lakes and
forests.

A little store sits at the bottom of the hillside. It is in an
old house by the highway at the end of Wood Lake.
Often I walk down there. When I come in coffee is
brewing. The owner gives me cookies. He gives me my
mail. Workers in boots and checkered jackets stand
around drinking coffee. They are gossiping. I learn
about the community at the corner store. The owner

named himself Nasty. In the long winter months I hear the gossip about my community at Nasty's.

In the summer the corner store is full of tourists. They are wet from jumping in the lake. They are hot and looking for an ice cream. Young couples in bathing suits will be sitting outside at the picnic tables, licking ice cream. Old couples will be wandering down the gravel road. Perhaps they are coming from the trailer camp.

People who live here are not burdened by poverty. They have come here with their life savings. They build houses in the hills where they can rest after long tiring lives in Vancouver or Calgary. If they are young they build houses in the hills and struggle to pay for them with odd jobs. They will be carpenters or construction workers or hostesses in restaurants. They are not rich but they have energy. They are possessive. They guard their plots of land and pieces of house with the fury of young ownership. If you offend them they never forgive you. It is a rural culture. Rural cultures are proud. They see their families expanding and their lands increasing and they are proud of themselves. If you come too close they bark like dogs. If you keep your distance they greet you pleasantly on the road.

Sometimes people like me come into the valley. People who want to be left alone. Who want to simply write a book or paint a picture. Grow vegetables, pick fruit, weave tapestries and watch hawks circling overhead in between. When those people come they move further north in the valley away from the millionaires in the south. You cannot find them unless you have contacts. Directions to their homes can only be had by word of mouth.

THIRTY

MY FRIEND HILLARY AND I DROVE TO THE NORTH OF THE valley. It was a warm summer day. As we drove, the landscape gently changed. The mountains became higher, the forests thicker and greener and darker. The air grew crisper. Instead of orchards with rows of fruit trees there were open pastures with lazy cows standing. It was not hard to sense that the Rocky Mountains were just beyond. We had lunch on a mountaintop. We felt the warmth of the sand at Mara Lake. We were watching everything and thinking everything.

We followed a sign on the road. The sign said ORGANI-CALLY GROWN CORN. Going down a side road into open fields we found an old house. From the driveway we could see the walls of the house loosening up, the windows rattling, the paint peeling off. It was old and uncared for. A young man with long hair came out. We said we wanted corn. He took us to the corn field and filled a bag for us. He told us he was on welfare for many years. Now he wanted to give something back to society. His wife was weeding the vegetable patch. She was thin. They were both thin. Their clothes were rags. They were poor. They were so poor the wind blew through them.

We paid for the bag of corn and took it home. That evening we boiled the cobs and had a corn dinner. It was especially good corn. There were moments of silence when we ate that supper. Something about the extreme poverty we witnessed put a rupture in the continuum of our thoughts.

I was thinking there are good people here too. I was hoping I would remember. I knew at times I would forget. Sometimes you are weary. You are so tired you think you cannot get any more tired. The water on the lake is gray. The sky is gray. The silence is severe. Then you remember the land gives. That golden gifts come out of the soil. They are meant for you. And you are to give them back to the world that made you.

THIRTY-ONE

"I AM SORRY I AM NOT IN MINNEAPOLIS WITH YOU TONIGHT. IF I were, I would phone you and then..." Jules said this in his ponderous manner. He spoke English slowly with a heavy French accent. As he spoke he slowly moved small objects from one spot to another on a surface, as though he were playing an important game of chess. I was thinking he would forget he said this. Already in the airplane he would have forgotten his former desire to be somewhere else. By that evening he would be in Montréal and I would be in Minneapolis and all the airplanes would have landed. It was irrevocable. But he was speaking and the words cut into the early morning air like the flight of a crow. Words that escape you rupture reality. They slice through the continuum of your existence and disappear. Your existence goes on. The words are gone. No one has overheard. But the cut the speaking made remains. Perhaps they were illicit words. Unofficial words. But they made a cut that cannot be covered. It is a language that escapes from its organic origins and when all is gone the rupture alone is left. The rupture is the text. I would have liked a text that covers the entire gash like smooth ointment. A wound on the skin. To know it can be healed over. But there is a scar instead. There for all to see. A textual scar perhaps. I was thinking of the crows of late winter in the barren orchards. They seat themselves on the gray pear trees standing stiffly. The crows gawk across the orchard. They are planning strategies. Where to place themselves when the first buds spring out, when the blossoms burst. When the first fruit of summer makes its appearance, how they will be placed at the precise moment. All I could do was smile because he knew I would be waiting if he were in Minneapolis. Perhaps a sad smile since it could not be done and it could not be spoken of and all wishful thoughts are fleeting. They dissipate like morning clouds rising in the heat of the sun. I thought it was just as well. Things are never what they seem. The more you know someone the less he appears like himself. The self you thought he was. People change every day. The things I know about him are not about the man with the eyes that are looking at me. He would not see in my eyes what he knows about me either. He would say no, *impossible*. He would look at me in that alarmed manner. He would hesitate as he scrutinized me again. My face would be calm. He would see nothing there. He would take a step back. There would be an alarmed hesitancy, the way it was when we met on an average afternoon with people all around. We shook hands and he stepped back in alarmed hesitancy. Something ripped. There was a tearing somewhere. "I will be sorry to separate from you," I ventured. His arm was around me and the morning was cold and the highway to Minneapolis was covered in tongues of snow and I was not looking forward to crossing the prairies. I would have liked to pause here longer. "It has to be done," Jules said slowly. Deliberately, a voice coming from far away, barely audible. And I was thinking it was just as well.

THIRTY-TWO

THAT NIGHT IN MINNEAPOLIS I SPENT INSTEAD WITH MY friends Jane and William. I drove across the prairie with William and on the way he bought a bottle of Benedictine. It was a large bottle. That evening he and Jane cooked lasagne and we talked. The bottle of Benedictine was opened. We were talking about adopted children. I told them a story about a girl and her three mothers. They told me about their children. They had both adopted children separately and raised them. Then the time came for the birth family to appear.

I thought I would not like to raise a child only to have it separate from me and go to the biological parent. It would be like watching your lover go back to his wife. Wondering in what way you exist. In what way am I real? What determines a real relationship? Is it length of time spent together? Twenty years together can be wiped out in one night. One error can erase twenty years of good family life. Is it official documents? If official documents make reality then emotions do not. Is reality determined by words on paper? If that is true then what I write is real. What I write exists. Unless it is written it does not exist. It never happened.

William's daughter found her biological brother. The incident was taped by the CBC and they met each other on the television screen for the first time. They can play the tape over and over. They can see themselves at the moment of their meeting. The hesitation. The desire to see and the fear to know. The hunger and hate. The love for alternate stories. What might have been. It is only chance that reality unfolded as it did. A piece of paper that says you are mine and not someone else's.

William told of the moment of their meeting. He sat at the table with the Benedictine in front of him. He was a large man with large hair and he wept. "You see, I can't even talk about it," he said. His face was weeping. What might have been. What is. My family that is not my family. Home is a place where you knock and enter at the same time. Uncertain of where you belong. A sense that you may be separating at any moment. The erosion of certainty. The wishful thought.

Jane listened to the story I told and exclaimed, "That's amazing. That's exactly my story." And I thought of how our stories interlap, overlap. How feelings are always the same. In every house emotions run parallel. How they build up and stay cloistered where you cannot see them. Then one day you meet someone and the shell cracks. There is a break somewhere. A tearing. Life cracks. Inside the cracks are amazing stories.

Stories of what you learn. How not to look behind you. Not to retrace your steps. To let the past be the past and the moment be the only moment. We undergo so many separations on so many levels. It is only because of your love that you notice the break. Only your desire lets you see the discontinuity. The separation has meaning only because you did not want it to take place.

THIRTY-THREE

THERE WERE OTHER TREES ON MY PROPERTY THAT I KNEW
would bear fruit but I did not know what kind. Below
my cottage was an open space ringed with various trees.
In the fall, after the apricots that came out first, I
inspected the rest of my fruitful holdings. It was a hot
day and the weeds and grasses I waded through were
dry and brittle.

When the gate was opened the first to appear was a
thick bush with bright red berries. They looked like
huckleberries or raspberries but were neither. The
berries hung wearily from the thin leggings of bush.
Farther down, along the northern fence, were
grapevines. The grapes were still green and young.
They hung firm and healthy, waiting for those magical

moments in late September when they could turn purple. When I read up on various grapes I found mine were the kind used in wine making. They were too sour to have as table grapes. I wondered if I would have time to make my own wine.

Below the grapevines stood a fine tall tree. Everywhere on its branches were little translucent yellow bulbs. It occurred to me they might be plums. I took one and ate it. The taste was sweet and succulent. They were yellow plums, hundreds of them. I got the blue buckets and filled them with plums. When they were carried to the house I sat and looked at my crop. It seemed like a miracle that I should have hundreds of plums, better than any I have ever tasted, coming as a gift unbargained for.

I discovered some peach trees below. They were old and had not been tended. Their branches meandered crookedly with awkward joints. The leaves were sometimes eaten through. But the peaches were fine and ripe. When I picked and tasted them I was again overwhelmed by the sweetness. Soon I had buckets of peaches as well. I had no idea what would become of all the fruit. In one corner of my land was an apple tree as well but the apples were beset by some pest that had bored holes in them. I left the tree alone. Later I would decide how to tend to it. Besides, I told myself, what would I do with another ten buckets of apples?
I remembered a time in my life when one could only

get such fruit by paying for it with the dearest of savings. All the visions in my memory of signs of malnutrition for lack of fruit were balking at the abundance around me as though my mind were playing tricks on me. Or perhaps reality was. The memories of hunger for this kind of food. Just precisely this. I did not recall ever having prayed for such a thing. But if I had I would have marveled at how prayers came true. But I never thought it was possible and saw no reason to bother God with the impossible.

THIRTY-FOUR

I WAS THINKING OF SPIRAL STAIRCASES. HOW THEY GO around gigantic water tanks or chimneys or towers or lighthouses. How you can go up or down the staircase and it does not matter where you are situated because the staircase goes nowhere and comes from nowhere. It is an empty construct with bars, clinging to nothing, left to totter by itself in the empty air. A railroad track pulled from the ground and made to spiral upward in circles. No train can follow those tracks anymore. The train would go over a cliff and be shattered in many pieces. I am climbing up such a staircase. It is a fire lookout at the top of a dry sandy mountain. There is no water on the mountain and the weeds and grasses and pine trees are brittle and dry. If a tinder were struck here, there would be forest fires and I am looking out for signs of smoke. I do not know why I am looking. There is no real reason for it. It has been a long climb and I forgot to bring water. I begin to ascend the staircase and feel the thinning air around me. I am struck by vertigo. The world below begins to swim. The brown and pale green hills are swimming. The lakes far below, blue as gems, are swimming. The crows gawking, the hawks circling. They are all floating and I think I will fall from this high place. I do not remember why I did not bring water. There are so many lakes down there and I brought no water. It would have been so easy to dip a flask in the lake and carry it on my back. I no longer remember why I have taken this hike. I do not see a man standing above at the top of the stairs. He is bending over and looking down at me. He may be wondering whether I will go all the way up or turn around. Or perhaps I will fall over and break in pieces on the ground below. Only in recollection do I see a man above. In reality I do not see him there. I do not know who he is or what he is thinking. He seems to come from another country and yet he does not. He is also very familiar but I do not know from where. My memories deceive me. He is wearing a large coat that seems to go down to his ankles. But I cannot see that well since he is above me and I have to strain my neck to look up. Straining my neck gives me vertigo and I am dizzy. I can see the coat is green. A pale mossy green like the pine trees in the early morning haze when the pines will not declare themselves. Yet you cannot deny they are there. If it is very dry they are dangerous. They might catch fire if a tinder is struck among them. I wonder why a frost is on the ground. There should not be frost. It is April and the winter should be gone but somehow it has returned. In the mornings I see the heavy veil of cloud among the hills, hovering over the lake. I know the clouds are full of snow. The fine little flakes are floating down effortlessly. The ground becomes dusted with them. The tops of the mountains are powdered with them. They are talking about the return of winter. How we have to traverse the highways through blowing tongues of snow. All the visions are melting in my mind because I am dizzy and I am trying to come down the spiral staircase. I have to report my findings and I do not know whom to report them to. Or for what reason. My report says I see no sign of smoke. There are no traces of anyone having been anywhere. No one would know we were there. Anyone coming after us would not notice we were there. If there are no consequences of us having been there then I can see we were never there. That is what I have in my report. Let us say no one was there.

THIRTY-FIVE

WHEN THE MORNING SUN IS BRIGHT LIKE THIS I FORGET IT
has been a harsh winter. There have been masses of
snow. Huge piles of snow have accumulated at my cottage door. The snow was as high as my waist. The
veranda around my cottage was weighted down too
heavily. The wooden pillars holding up so many tons of
snow were about to break. I took a snow shovel and
pushed all the snow away. It took many days to get the
snow off the veranda. The road was snowed in and I
could not drive down to the cottage. I had to park the
car above, on the hillside, and wade through the snow
in boots that were never tall enough.

Now that the snow has melted it is hard to remember it
was ever there. The ice on the lake has melted. The water
jiggles nervously in the early sunlight. Millions of tiny

dots of light flicker on the surface. It is like the most nervous traffic jam. All the little fireflies are rushing around.

·

The veil of the morning has been lifted. The clouds have dissipated and become a morning haze. The haze filters everything. The mountainside opposite the lake is bathed in haze. It is hard to tell where the woodland ends and the open pastures begin. Where the orchards end and the lake begins. All melts into one. There is only a change of color where the mountain meets the sky. A wooded darkness meets a thin lightness.

·

Then the glitter of the morning is gone. Dogs begin to bark angrily. Women begin to pick gravel on the road. Girls are out gathering pine cones in the forest. Men are hammering together walls. I can hear the hammer blows in the distance. Workers are picking up dead branches littering the orchards. They were pruning all the trees in the final months of winter and branches lie scattered as though a wind had swept through and all the trees had broken.

I know there is all this work to be done and I know I am tired. I think I can hardly get more tired and then I do. I think the spring will come with blossoms and I will rest in the sun. All my memories will run together and I will be glad they do.

THIRTY-SIX

I AM THE PLACE FROM WHICH THE VOICE IS HEARD, JACQUES Lacan said. *This place is called Jouissance*. There is nothing here to be seen. It is the empty space where the breath breaks through. It is a wind in a tunnel, strong enough to fell whole trees with shallow root systems. There is no Other for this *jouissance* unless it be through desire. I cannot prove that the Other exists unless it be by loving him.

We are trapped in images not of our choosing. We have come a long way only to find that we went nowhere. We came all this way from the apple tree only to find another apple tree. The apples here are falling before they can be picked. It is because the tree has been neglected and the worms have feasted on the fruit. The apples lying on the ground are riddled with holes. They have been rotting in the grass and the bees have found them.

In the valley where I live the fruit farmers complain about their apple orchards. They say apple trees are the worst. Apple trees attract infestations. They have to be sprayed every season. In the early summer you can see sprayers in the orchards. They are people who appear to have landed in a spaceship. They are outfitted in protective clothing. Their faces covered in masks. They make you think of the war in the Persian Gulf when everyone put gas masks on. In their hands they hold devices from which a hard poisonous spray covers the fruit.

The world has a device it can use to hold me hostage. It is a device of organic symbols where they say words are coming from. In my joy I am illicit. My joy itself is forbidden because no document has sanctioned it. The universe is a defect. I myself am a defect. The cosmos would be purer without me. And that is what I am trying to say. I am trying to say it is the defect that matters. You know you exist because there is a break, a problem. Because something has been forbidden and it is so hard to believe.

Laughter itself is the breath of the mistake. A defection from the rule of tyrants. Because there were iron curtains everywhere and you saw a break in them where the daylight filtered in. In the blue light of dawn you saw clearly the man lying beside you. He was sleeping and you saw whom you had been with. Suddenly there were no tyrants. There were no dictators and the curtain had broken. The veil had been torn and in the tearing of the veil you saw his face imprinted. The face was clearly there. A shadow cast into your world and you were laughing.

Because when you arise in the early dawn you recognize that the unspeakable has laid hands on you. In the unspeakable there has been a blessing. A gift in the palm of his hand. He transferred the gift to you when he placed the palm of his hand on your body. A gift of language. Of accidental joy.

You want to say you are not trapped in these images of valleys and mountains, of canyons and peaks. Of streams and bridges, of towers and ruptures and spiral staircases. That like a circling hawk you can fly beyond them all. They cannot hold you.

It will be much easier now to see the airplane land in the valley. To watch my bags coming out a trapdoor in the wall, floating forward on a conveyor belt. To drive to my cottage and see that the ice on the lake has melted. The ice fishermen are gone. The ducks are swimming freely. A boat is on the water. The iron hold of winter has loosened. The bars are falling off. Their joints are weakened and they collapse at a touch.

THIRTY-SEVEN

IT IS A FAMOUS SAYING THAT PARTING IS SUCH SWEET SORROW. As sweet as the plums I accidentally discovered growing on my property. A stately tree holding hundreds of golden plums. They were crisp ripe fruits filled with the golden nectar that was once said to come from the gods. I remember sitting on my veranda wondering what to do with all the plums. How could I keep them from rotting once they had been picked. And how surprised I was that the fruit kept so fresh. Time went on and on and the fruit remained fresh.

There were no words. There could not have been any words. There was nothing to say yet the air was filled with what remained unspoken. Perhaps a clasping of fingers. A touching of elbows. A meeting of lips. Knowing our languages were touching for the last time. A parting.

I went in to get my bag because it was time to go. Someone had left me a basket of fruit. The wicker basket stood there waiting to be taken along. It was filled with grapes, bananas, apples, oranges. I took the basket in my hand and came down to the car that was to take me across the prairies to Minneapolis. I would catch an airplane for my valley in the British Columbia mountains. There was no sign of Jules at the door. He had disappeared into thin air.

When William and I drove across the prairie the wind blew with a certain fury. Tongues of snow flew across our path. It had been snowing overnight and the fields were white again. Winter had returned and it was unexpected. As we approached Minnesota the snow thinned out. We saw it had only been snowing on the Dakota side. We stopped and William bought his bottle of Benedictine.

I was looking south while I waited for him to reemerge with his bottle of golden liquid. The fields were there, which in summer would be blue and yellow with flax and wheat. A railroad track cut through them. Over the tracks, at regular intervals, a long train with many boxcars slid forward with an alarming noise. From a distance the train looked like a slow snake spewing a little

smoke as it went. The body of boxes wound itself clum-
sily around the bend with the tracks. One huge headlight blasted from the front engine. An overcast haze
was in the air. Anyone walking on the tracks would find
the sound of the train muffled by the falling snow.
Would be uncertain what was coming was the headlight
of a train or the sun buried in a veil of thin cloud.

Perhaps it has been a sad laughter all along. A sadness
infused with the joy of morning.

THIRTY-EIGHT

I HAVE A COTTAGE IN THE OKANAGAN VALLEY. I LIVE HERE because I can repeat myself as often as I desire. Nothing will come of all my repetitions. Every summer I can watch blossoms come and go on fruit trees. I can see tulips spring out and geraniums grow and corn become tall. I can see beans in a row. Grapevines in a row. Raspberries in a row. Every autumn I can fill buckets with fruit and watch them turn into jam and chutney and pies.

I live here because here I can make all the mistakes I desire. All I will hear will be joyful laughter. There are no censors here. There are only dark blue mornings when the lake water is blank and the mountain tries to find its own vain reflection when the early clouds have lifted. Your mistakes define you. To be censored from your mistakes is to be censored from yourself. I do not want to wander across the cold prairie looking for myself. Trying to catch my vain reflection in the dropping snow.

My cottage is on the mountainside. I can see far and wide from my home. I can see hawks hovering, crows circling, ducks gliding in the water. I can see a solitary rowboat making waves on the lake. See where the prow parts the water and where it closes behind the keel. I can see trucks filled with fruit in autumn on their way to market. The first purple flowers of spring and the falling leaves of autumn.

Because it is my pleasure to live here. Because it is the place of *jouissance* that is censored yet binding. Only your moments of pleasure can stand for the string that holds the grapevines up for the sun to see. It is *pleasure as that which binds incoherent life together*, Jacques Lacan said. All my incoherent years are held up by the pleasure of being here. By the dew on the grasses, the wind in the ponderosas, the grapes on the vine.

Here my thoughts become a pool of water, blank and sleek in the morning sun. Here I can see a host of fruitful moments reflecting themselves. I think warm thoughts. I remember warm people. My reflections will not be torn away from me by Stalinist historians who wish to rewrite my stories. Embarrassed historians, obsessive historians, proper historians. My improper thoughts can be left to themselves. There will be memories of hawks circling in ever-growing spirals, climbing their joy.

THIRTY-NINE

I WAS GLAD TO SEE MY LIFE COME BACK TO ME. GLAD TO SEE THE slow-moving trucks bounce up the potholed gravel road to my cottage. They were bringing all the objects of my discordant life that had been strewn about the continent. Objects from lives I had lent to others in my vain attempts to live properly. To bow to the censor's blue lines and to lose myself in those lines. I thought it would make others happy but it made no one happy. It only created more blue lines. I noticed that the blue lines would never stop being drawn.

I noticed a fear of death. That if you die in the blue line then no one has died because no one was there. A fear of non-being. A non-being that has to be broken. To exist it appeared I had to make myself defective. To make my own mistakes. In my mistakes I can find the pleasure of being.

Brass beds and wicker chairs and oak tables came out of the moving trucks and into my cottage. Objects long forgotten. Pictures of boats and shepherds. Posters of events. Boots and jackets. Hundreds of books came into my cottage library. Plants still blooming in spite of colossal neglect. Records I could still play. Cups and pots and plates with no cracks in spite of all the transportation. Children's books with children's stories and children's memories. A number of things I had forgotten.

I was glad to see my life come back to me. To be able to say I did this. For better or worse I did this. These are my mistakes. The illicit moments. The improper moments. Because I rejoiced in life I bought more objects, read more books, wrote more words. I cleared the leaves of last year away. Cleared the weeds that had grown and hardened into straw. I swept the dust from the veranda and the porch and the driveway. I pruned the apricot trees and weeded the vegetable patch.

It is so much easier now to be in love outside the iron grid and the paper sanctions. To be illicitly in love without a single ripple on the water's surface. To read familiarity in the face of a stranger. To recognize myself in the unknown. To understand another language for the first time.

FORTY

"WHENEVER I GO TO A PLACE FOR THE FIRST TIME, I KNOW I will always come back." When Jules said that, his jacket was slung over this shoulder in the heat of the day. The Pacific Ocean furrowed itself behind him. I could see freighters sailing toward the deep sea. Buskers on the sidewalk. An old man playing the flute by the harbor. A juggler in a side street casting for pennies. I thought he must be right. There is no end to this chance meeting. Chance meetings continue to occur. They happen all over the country and it is always the same person. It is impossible to be anonymous, to remain strangers. Nothing is ever new. The words we use to speak to each other are loaded. Analysts have looked into the words and found baggage there. They carry our desires, our violence, our love. *All discourse has its effect through the unconscious*, Jacques Lacan said. He was speaking of *the supreme narcissism of the Lost Cause.* I was thinking of Jules' deliberate ponderous way of walking. Of the story of the lost cause. Trying to imagine a story that is not a lost cause. I love the story because it cannot end and it cannot go on. We are suspended in the string of our desire like a spider hanging from its web. The spider is lowering itself from the balcony slowly and it will never reach the ground. There is no ground below. There is only a perpetual descent into an unknown depth. It is night and we are in a beautiful Pacific city and Jules says, "What we are living now is fiction." There is a recognition that the body has its own technique. Its own story. Its own fiction. We can try to make sense of the fiction of the body but the thread continues to elude us. The subject vanishes around the corner just as we think we have caught sight of him. A recognition that *we make ourselves the instruments of each other's jouissance.* We cannot do without each other and we do not want each other at the same time. I find I can sit on the grass in the park and listen to a string quartet play Haydn. I forget Jules is standing a few paces away, his jacket slung over his shoulder. This is his country and he is in a foreign country at the same time. No one here speaks French. They refuse to speak French here the way they refuse to speak English to me in Montréal. It is all a refusal. If I lie down on the grass I will bake in the spring sun. There will be hundreds of people around me in the park and I will bake in the sun repetitiously. When my eyes are open I will see Jules standing a few paces away, towering above me.

FORTY-ONE

I WOULD SAY I AM TIRED. WINTER HAS BEEN LONG AND SPRING has been slow. I no longer know what I have to do. Work that is made for me piles up. I have confused it with work I want to do.

I have begun to stare at the lights on the mountain at night. On the other side of the lake lights are scattered where people live. The lights are reflected in the lake. All the ice has melted and strings of light can be seen on the water. When the moon is full there is a wide band of moonlight on the water as well. In the country the air is clear and all the stars are visible. The lights of the lake and the lights of the mountain are met by the lights in the sky. Everywhere the world sparkles at night, like the sun sparkling itself in the water during the day.

From my cottage I see shooting stars. They pass over-head at great speed, going from south to north. They are moments flashing across the night sky. Then they are gone.

In the spring, before the leaves are on the trees, the early mornings are noisy. Hundreds of different birds are calling out the daylight hours. I do not know what half of them are. There are more birds than I imagined. They are delighted at the prospect of blossoming orchards and clear blue lake water and tiny red leaves on little plum trees. The grass has become bright green. The blue haze has settled over everything.

I am thinking home is where you choose to forget and choose to remember at the same time. Nothing hinders your choices. Nothing forces you to remember and nothing forces you to forget. There is no reason to repress any memory. There is no reason to hold it up against the daylight either.

And I shall have some peace there, for peace comes dropping slow,
Dropping from the veils of the morning....
—W.B. YEATS,
"The Lake Isle of Innisfree"